MARGIT: BOOK FOUR

A FRIEND
IN NEED

KATHY KACER

**Look for the other Margit stories
in Our Canadian Girl**

Book One: Home Free

Book Two: A Bit of Love and a Bit of Luck

Book Three: Open Your Doors

Margit: Book Four

A FRIEND IN NEED

KATHY KACER

PENGUIN
CANADA

PENGUIN CANADA

Published by the Penguin Group

Penguin Group (Canada), 90 Eglinton Avenue East, Suite 700, Toronto, Ontario, Canada M4P 2Y3
(a division of Pearson Canada Inc.)

Penguin Group (USA) Inc., 375 Hudson Street, New York, New York 10014, U.S.A.
Penguin Books Ltd, 80 Strand, London WC2R 0RL, England
Penguin Ireland, 25 St Stephen's Green, Dublin 2, Ireland (a division of Penguin Books Ltd)
Penguin Group (Australia), 250 Camberwell Road, Camberwell, Victoria 3124, Australia
(a division of Pearson Australia Group Pty Ltd)
Penguin Books India Pvt Ltd, 11 Community Centre, Panchsheel Park, New Delhi – 110 017, India
Penguin Group (NZ), 67 Apollo Drive, Rosedale, North Shore 0632, New Zealand
(a division of Pearson New Zealand Ltd)
Penguin Books (South Africa) (Pty) Ltd, 24 Sturdee Avenue, Rosebank, Johannesburg 2196,
South Africa

Penguin Books Ltd, Registered Offices: 80 Strand, London WC2R 0RL, England

First published 2007

1 2 3 4 5 6 7 8 9 10   (WEB)

Manufactured in Canada.

Library and Archives Canada Cataloguing in Publication data available upon request.

ISBN-13: 978-0-14-305116-9
ISBN-10: 0-14-305116-4

Visit the Penguin Group (Canada) website at **www.penguin.ca**

Special and corporate bulk purchase rates available; please see
www.penguin.ca/corporatesales or call 1-800-810-3104, ext. 477 or 474

For my nieces and nephews,

with love

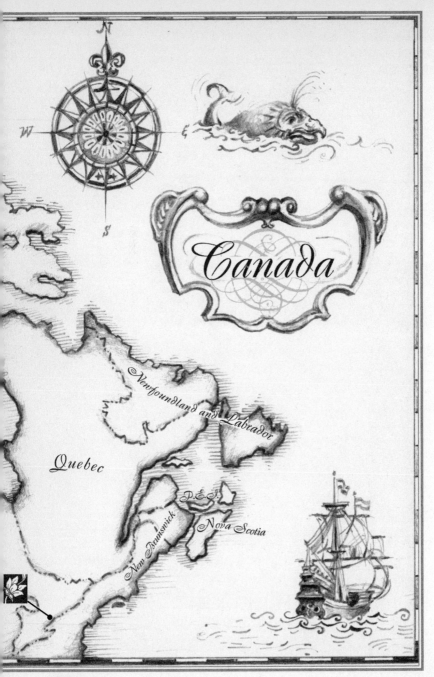

Canada

Quebec

Newfoundland and Labrador

P.E.I.

Nova Scotia

New Brunswick

Marks the location of the story

MARGIT'S NEW FAMILY

It is now 1947, and two years have passed since World War II ended. During the war, the Jewish community in Canada tried, with little success, to convince the Canadian government to admit Jewish refugees, those who were seeking a safe country in which to live. But now, two years later, Canada has finally agreed to open its doors to a group of Jewish orphans whose parents have died or been killed at the hands of Adolf Hitler and his Nazi armies. Between 1947 and 1949, 1,123 Jewish orphans will be admitted into Canada as part of the War Orphans Project of the Canadian Jewish Congress. The orphans will come from fifteen different countries across Europe. Seven hundred and eighty-three of these youngsters have survived concentration camps, the prison camps that were established by Adolf Hitler during the war to torture and kill Jews. The remaining 229 orphans have survived the war in hiding.

When these children arrive in Canada, they will be dispersed across the country. The majority of them— 798 in total—will be sent to live in Toronto and Montreal. One hundred and thirty-one orphans are sent to Manitoba, thirty-eight to British Columbia, twenty-eight to Alberta, and twelve to Saskatchewan.

Jewish communities across Canada have worked tirelessly to find foster homes, schools, and other services for these orphans. Boards of education will provide special classes, doctors and dentists have offered health care, social workers are in place to give support, and families have come forward to open their homes to these young survivors of the war.

The Jewish children who arrive in Canada at this time have lost everything and everybody. Many are unable to shake off the horror of their wartime experiences. Some are rebellious and display strange behaviours like hoarding food. Others run away from their foster families and are suspicious and mistrusting of anyone who has offered help. Some will even have to be moved about to several homes before they can find a place where they can finally settle. At the time of their arrival in Canada, it is unknown, given their trauma, whether these young survivors will adjust to their new lives.

Margit has managed to convince her family to take in nine-year-old Lilly, a young orphan from Poland.

Margit is jubilant and dreams that this young girl will become a good friend. But Lilly is distant and scared. She rejects every attempt that Margit makes to befriend her. Margit is trying to be patient, but she is also frustrated by Lilly's reluctance to trust her. And on top of this, Lilly's presence is jeopardizing Margit's friendship with her best friend, Alice. Will Margit be able to help Lilly adjust to life in Canada? Will Lilly become the friend and sister that Margit hopes for? And will Margit ever be able to repair her relationship with Alice?

CHAPTER N°. 1

"We're home, Lilly," Margit *called out* over her shoulder as she ran up the stairs of the small two-storey building. She reached the landing on the second floor and paused to turn and gaze down the staircase behind her. A small girl slowly made her way up the narrow flight of stairs. She moved up each step, carefully and silently, her head down, hardly making a sound, placing one foot in front of the other. Her straight brown hair hung over her downcast eyes, making it even more diffi-cult to see *her pale face.* She wore a faded green coat, and she clutched a big doll in her arms,

shifting it slightly from side to side, so that its legs would not bang against the stairs. The doll practically dwarfed the nine-year-old girl.

"Hurry up, Lilly," Margit called out once more. Margit was trying to be patient, but this was taking too much time. Besides, there was so much she wanted to show Lilly—so much she wanted to tell her. Lilly had been so quiet on the train ride from Halifax.

"We will be in Toronto very soon," Margit had said, speaking slowly and pronouncing each word carefully. "To-ron-to." Lilly had stared at Margit and said nothing.

"This is a train," Margit tried again, pointing around her. "Can you say 'train'?" No answer.

Margit had tried everything to engage Lilly in conversation during the long train trip from the East Coast. She had tried reading stories to her, she sang songs, she drew pictures—all to no avail. Lilly had sat in silence. It didn't help that Lilly spoke no English and Margit did not know a word of Polish, Lilly's mother tongue. Still,

She had tried reading stories to her, she sang songs, she drew pictures—all to no avail. Lilly had sat in silence.

Margit had hoped that Lilly might at least make an effort to talk to her—to try a few new words, or to respond to Margit's simple questions.

"I don't know what else to do," Margit had complained quietly to her father, who sat next to the girls in the train, watching thoughtfully.

"Be patient with Lilly," Papa had said. "It will take a long time for her to feel comfortable with us. Try to remember how long it took you to adjust to life here in Canada when you first came."

Margit had sat back in her seat. Papa was right, as usual, she thought. When Margit had arrived in Toronto from Czechoslovakia, almost three years earlier, in 1944, she had been just like Lilly—a frightened little girl who had escaped a terrible war in Europe, a war that had singled out Jewish people like Margit and Lilly. Margit had managed to escape from Europe with her mother. Papa had joined them later. Lilly's circumstances were even more difficult. She had survived the war in Poland. But her parents were dead—killed in one of the concentration camps where so many Jewish people had been tortured and killed. Margit didn't know all of Lilly's story, how she had survived and where. Papa knew some of these answers but had said very little.

"All in good time," he said. "The important thing is that Lilly is safe and here with us."

Safe, yes, thought Margit. *But* so *quiet.* This was not at all what Margit had expected when she had convinced her parents to provide a home for this little orphan girl. Margit sighed. *Maybe when Lilly gets to my home, she'll begin to relax and talk.* Margit wanted Lilly to see the apartment where she and her family lived. She wanted this little girl to begin to make friends with her—to begin to act like the sister Margit hoped she would be.

Lilly finally reached the top of the landing, where Margit stood waiting for her. Margit's hand trembled as she placed the key in the lock, turned the knob, and opened the door. "Welcome to your new home, Lilly," Margit said, motioning Lilly to follow her into the apartment. Mamma and Jack were waiting inside.

"I'm so glad you're home," Mamma exclaimed, hugging Margit tightly. Mamma reached down and took Lilly's hand in hers, stroking it gently and looking deeply into Lilly's eyes. "*Witamy w naszym domu.* Welcome to our home."

Lilly looked up briefly, surprised that Mamma knew some words of Polish. The small girl opened her mouth, and Margit thought that finally Lilly was going to speak. But before anything could come out, Jack charged into Margit's arms, jumping up and down and clapping his hands. "Mah-git!" he exclaimed. "Park." Jack wrapped his chubby arms tightly around Margit's neck and squeezed with all his might. Margit laughed and struggled to free herself from Jack's grasp.

"I'm happy to see you too, Jack," said Margit. "We'll go to the park later, but come meet Lilly." Margit turned Jack around, and with her own arm extended his hand to hold Lilly's. "Jack, this is Lilly. Can you say *'Lilly'?*"

Jack cocked his head to one side, eying the young stranger who stood so solemnly in front of him. "Dibby," said Jack finally. Margit stifled a laugh and looked over at Lilly. Was it Margit's imagination, or did Lilly smile the briefest of smiles? Her eyes seemed to soften as she looked down at Jack and held on to his hand. Then, just as quickly, it was over, and Lilly became sombre once more.

"Well," said Mamma, taking charge of the situation. "Margit, I want you to help Lilly get unpacked. Show her where to put her things and where she will be sleeping. I'm going to finish preparing supper and when the two of you are done, we'll sit down to eat." Mamma turned to Lilly. *"Zaraz będziemy, jeść.* We will eat soon." Then she picked up Jack and headed for the kitchen with Papa following.

Margit turned back to Lilly. "Well, here we are," she said. "This is where you're going to be sleeping." Margit pointed to the pullout couch in the living room. "I know it isn't much and it isn't very private, but I think it's comfortable." Lilly stared at Margit. "Bed," said Margit. "Sleep." Lilly's silence was becoming unbearable. This was harder than Margit had imagined. But she wasn't about to stop trying. *I won't give up*, she said to herself. *It's just going to take time, that's all.* She picked up Lilly's suitcase and placed it on the couch. Lilly moved closer as Margit opened the suitcase and peered inside. There was hardly anything there—a couple of skirts, one or two blouses, a sweater, some socks and underwear. The clothes were new, obviously given to Lilly by the people at the Canadian Jewish Congress, the group that had helped bring Lilly and the other orphans to Canada. Margit shook her head. She was overcome with sadness that Lilly had so few things. There were no toys, no special belongings—nothing but a few clean pieces of clothing.

Margit sighed and began to carry the clothes over to the closet in the living room, where her family kept their coats. Papa had built a couple of shelves off to one side where Lilly could put her things. Within no time, the suitcase was emptied and the clothes were stacked on one shelf. Margit was just about to close the suitcase when, suddenly, Lilly grabbed her arm.

"What's wrong?" Margit asked, startled by Lilly's action.

Lilly reached into a side pocket of the suitcase and pulled out a photograph. She stared down at it, rubbing her hand across the photo as if she were stroking the faces of the people posed there. Over Lilly's shoulder, Margit could see the faded picture of a girl, a woman, and a man. Margit recognized Lilly as the little girl in the photo. It looked like it had been taken a few years earlier. Lilly continued to gaze at the family in the picture, touching it and holding it close to her face. Then she looked up at Margit and said the first word she had spoken since arriving.

"*Mamusia.*"

CHAPTER N.º 2

"Mamusia," Lilly repeated, holding up the photo to show Margit.

Margit stared at the picture, mesmerized by this family who posed, smiling, for the camera. "Mother," Margit murmured. "It's your mother, isn't it, Lilly?"

Lilly nodded. "*Moja mamusia,*" she said again, more softly. "*Papa.*" Lilly touched the picture one more time and then carefully placed it on a small table next to the couch.

Margit did not know what to say. Everything she had wanted to show Lilly seemed so insignificant now as she watched this small, sad girl place her single most precious possession next to the place where she would be sleeping. Margit sighed, reached for Lilly's hand, and headed for the kitchen.

Later that afternoon, Margit left the apartment with Jack to go to the park. The afternoon was hot. The July sun beat down on Margit's head, and only a few steps into their walk the sweat was pouring down Margit's face as she firmly clutched Jack's hand and crossed Dundas Street heading to Alexandra Park. This was the closest park to Margit's home, and Jack loved it the most, particularly its wading pool. Though he was only two years of age, Jack practically knew the way to the park by himself. He walked steps ahead of Margit, tugging on her hand. "Fast," he insisted. Margit was distracted with thoughts of Lilly, and absently followed Jack's lead. Once inside the park, Jack broke free of Margit's grip. Alice was already there, waiting impatiently for her friend Margit to arrive.

"Where is she?" Alice cried as she greeted Margit. "Why didn't you bring her?"

"Lilly's resting," Margit replied. Lilly had been so exhausted that her head had practically fallen onto the table during the meal that Mamma had prepared. Finally, Mamma had guided Lilly to the couch. Lilly was fast asleep even before Mamma had a chance to lift her feet onto the couch and cover her with a soft blanket. It was Mamma's idea for Margit to take Jack to the park and let Lilly sleep in peace. Jack had been delighted.

"Dibby sleep," Jack explained to Alice, before running off to the water. He quickly stripped off his shoes and socks and waded into the shallow pool, splashing water into the air with his feet. Margit and Alice sat down on a shady stretch of grass next to the concrete pond where they could watch Jack and talk. The park was full of families on this summer afternoon. Young children played in the pool. Their parents sat on benches close by, watching and supervising the activity, periodically calling out to their youngsters. The humidity hung thick in the air. Everything felt heavy and lazy.

"So, tell me," said Alice. "What is she like?"

Margit wiped the sweat from her upper lip and shrugged her shoulders. "I don't know, Alice. Lilly's quiet and sad. She hasn't said a word, not on the whole trip from Halifax or anything. She just stares at all of us. I've tried to talk to her, but she doesn't answer me. I've tried to teach her some English words, but she won't even try to say anything. This is so much harder than I thought it would be."

Alice nodded her head. "I'm sure it must be hard for Lilly. I mean, she doesn't know any of you, she doesn't have any family, and she doesn't speak any English."

"But it's hard for me too," cried Margit. "I mean … I know it's hard for Lilly, but I want so much for her to be my friend. She isn't even trying."

Alice looked thoughtful. "Just think about how strange all of this must be for her," Alice said, "and scary. Remember when you first arrived here in Toronto and we met in the market? You didn't know any English, you didn't have any friends, and everything was new and confusing for you. You were pretty scared too."

Alice was so smart and thoughtful, and Margit admired that in her. Those first few days in Toronto had been terrifying for Margit. Alice had been the first person Margit had met when she and her mother were out walking in Kensington Market, the area of Toronto where they had settled and where they now lived. Margit and Alice had become instant friends. Alice had patiently taught Margit her first words of English. She had sat next to Margit in school and helped her with her subjects. Alice taught Margit what to wear and how to fit in. She introduced Margit to other friends, and even stood up for her when Margit needed help. Margit could not imagine what her life in Toronto would have been like without Alice by her side. "I do know how hard it is when you feel different," Margit said. "But when I first came to Toronto, I was so happy that you were here to be my friend. Lilly doesn't seem to notice me. I'm not even sure she likes me."

Alice laughed and nudged her friend. "Of course she likes you. I have an idea. I'll come by your place tomorrow. The three of us can go to the market, and I'll show Lilly my parents' store, just like I showed you when you first arrived." Alice's parents owned a flower shop in the market. Some of the first words of English that Margit had learned had been the names of flowers.

But Margit shook her head. "No thanks," she said. "I want to spend time alone with Lilly. If *this* is going to work, then I've got to do *this* myself. I'll take Lilly somewhere special tomorrow— maybe the library, or I'll show her our school." Margit looked up in time to catch the hurt look on Alice's face. It startled her. Why would Alice be upset about Margit's plan? Surely she understood the importance of Margit and Lilly's spending time together. Margit shook her head. She didn't have time to worry about Alice right now. She had more important things on her mind. She had work to do with Lilly, and she knew it was going to be a big job.

That night at dinner, Lilly sat sombrely with her head bowed, avoiding eye contact with Margit and her parents. But when the food was brought to the table, she suddenly came alive. She piled her plate high with food: four pieces of chicken, a mound of carrots, and three slices of bread. When she thought no one was looking, she quickly snuck one extra slice of bread and pushed it deep into her pocket. Margit watched with her mouth open. If she had taken this much food, her mother would have scolded her. "Margit," she would have said, "your eyes are bigger than your stomach. Do you think the food is free?" But Mamma said nothing. She stroked Lilly's head and offered her more to eat. Lilly's eyes widened as if she had not seen this much food in the longest time, or as if she was not accustomed to this kind of generosity.

Jack sat next to Lilly, watching with enjoyment as Lilly continued to pile food onto her plate. "Dibby, eat," he commanded, before shovelling a forkful of mashed potatoes into his own mouth. "Mmm, good." Potato oozed out of the corners of Jack's mouth. This seemed to amuse him even more. He smacked his lips together and squealed with delight.

Lilly reached over to touch Jack's fingers. She stroked them gently before withdrawing her hand. Jack laughed again. "Tickle," he said, reaching over to touch Lilly's hand.

Margit looked on enviously. It was so simple for Jack. All he had to do was giggle and talk in his baby talk, and everyone around him would jump hoops to amuse him, including Lilly. Jack seemed to be the only one who could bring a smile to Lilly's lips. If only it were that easy for Margit.

"What is it, Margitka? You haven't touched your dinner. Are you not feeling well?" Papa's questions interrupted Margit's thoughts.

"I'm fine, Papa," she said. "I'm just thinking about Lilly. She showed me a picture earlier today, a picture of her parents. I think it's the only thing she has of them."

Margit and her parents quickly lowered their voices and began to talk in hushed tones. They spoke in Czech, as they always did when it was just the three of them, lowering their voices as if they didn't want Lilly to hear what they were saying, even though she was sitting right there. In fact, they could have been shouting out loud. Lilly didn't understand a word of their conversation, but more importantly, she didn't seem to care that they were talking.

Papa nodded. "Yes, I believe you are right. Lilly's parents were arrested early on in the war.

They were sent to Auschwitz. You know about Auschwitz, don't you, Margit?" Papa shook his head and closed his eyes as he talked. "Of all of Hitler's concentration camps, this was among the worst. So many Jews were killed there, so many treated inhumanely."

Papa paused. Margit knew that it was painful for him to talk about this. He had been in one of those concentration camps himself—arrested just before Margit and her mother managed to escape from their home in Czechoslovakia and make it out of Europe. He had been lucky to survive and join his family in Canada at the end of the war. But the memory of that time still tore at Papa's heart.

"What happened to her parents, Papa?" Margit asked softly. She had to know the answer to this question. If she had any hope of getting close to Lilly, she had to understand what Lilly had gone through.

Papa took a deep breath and wiped his eyes before continuing. "The documents say that they were killed as soon as they arrived in Auschwitz.

Before their arrest, they managed to leave Lilly with a neighbour, someone who said she would protect Lilly and keep her safe. It was very dangerous for both of them. So Lilly was kept hidden away, where no one could see her."

Papa sat back in his chair. Talking about that time always left Papa weak with sadness and despair. Mamma placed a hand on his shoulder and continued the story. "There were Christians who protected Jews during that time. They were the ones willing to risk their lives to help their Jewish friends and neighbours. If more had been willing to do this, perhaps the outcome of the war would have been very different for our people."

"Even though this neighbour protected her, I don't think Lilly ever felt safe," Papa added. "There was little food to eat and always the worry that soldiers would come looking for her. At the end of the war, the neighbour brought Lilly to a Jewish agency. Lilly was malnourished and weak."

"You can understand why Lilly takes so much food onto her plate," Mamma continued, as if reading Margit's mind. "Lilly must be thinking that this will all disappear again—that she will be left with nothing to eat. She doesn't believe that she can trust us, yet."

Across the table, Jack and Lilly were still playing their little game. Jack would place his arm on the table and wait. Lilly's fingers tiptoed across the table and up Jack's arm. Each time, Jack responded with a fit of laughter. "More, Dibby," he said, placing his hand on the table again.

Margit searched Lilly's face as if she were seeing this young girl for the very first time— her fleeting smile, her haunted eyes, her colourless cheeks. Margit had been so quick to judge Lilly's silence as indifference or coldness. Perhaps Lilly had just forgotten what it was like to be in a loving family, and how to return affection. She had forgotten what it was like to trust someone. Margit felt a new resolve. *I will be more patient*, Margit vowed to herself. *I'll show Lilly that she can depend on us, that she can feel safe here.*

CHAPTER N°. 4

It took Margit a long time to fall asleep that night. All she could think about was the photo of Lilly and her parents. They had looked so happy in the picture, smiling and holding on to one another in a loving embrace. Lilly's face was innocent and happy, as if she could never imagine that her family could be taken away from her. It was hard for Margit to see Lilly as she looked today—scared and suspicious. *But who can blame her,* wondered Margit. *Everything in Lilly's life has changed. Everything has been taken from her.* Margit knew that Lilly had endured more sadness

24

in her nine short years than most people experienced in a lifetime.

Margit tossed and turned for what seemed like hours and finally drifted into a fitful sleep. It felt like only minutes had passed when she was suddenly startled awake by a noise—a muffled, scraping sound that felt as if it was next to her. Margit's bedroom was separated from the living room by a curtain that Mamma had hung there. In her family's cramped living quarters, this curtain provided a cozy private bedroom space. But she heard all the noises from the apartment, especially from the living room on the other side of the curtain. Margit rubbed her eyes and tried to focus in the darkness. A truck rumbled by along the street below the apartment. Its engine sputtered and popped, then the sound slowly faded as the truck moved on around the next corner. Margit listened again. Perhaps it had been a dream that had awakened her, or maybe Jack was talking in his sleep, as he sometimes did from the bedroom where he still slept with their parents. Margit lay still on her bed, trying to concentrate. There it was again—first some scratching, then a gentle swishing noise and a soft thud. There was no mistaking it. The noise was coming directly from the living room where Lilly slept.

Margit pushed her thin blanket aside and stepped onto the floor, shivering in spite of the summer heat that hovered in the apartment. She tiptoed cautiously to her bedroom curtain, took a deep breath, and peered around to the other side. Margit didn't know what time it was, but from the grey shadows that hung across the ceiling and floor, she knew that it had to be the middle of the night. Everything was still. Aside from the gentle buzz of Papa snoring from the bedroom, there were no other sounds in the apartment. Had she imagined the noise? Margit didn't think she had. She paused and listened once more, but there was only silence. Margit sighed. Perhaps she had dreamed it after all. She was just about to return to her bed when she glanced over at the couch, straining to make out Lilly's shape in the bed that had been pulled out from the sofa. And then Margit froze. There was no blanket, no pillow, and no Lilly.

In a flash, Margit was next to the couch, touching the sheet as if the darkness could have somehow hidden Lilly from her view. She fell to her knees and groped underneath the couch. Had Lilly fallen off the bed? Was she stuck beneath the sofa? Frantically, Margit felt the floor in all directions, but Lilly wasn't there. She stood up, breathing deeply and anxiously. Then she darted over to the bathroom. The door was open, but Lilly was not inside. Then Margit ran into the kitchen. Perhaps Lilly had wanted water, or tea. The beam of a street lamp streamed through the small window above the sink. It cast a long tunnel of light across the kitchen floor and up one wall. Margit's eyes searched everywhere. There was no sign of Lilly.

By now Margit was sweating. The hot air in the apartment was stifling. That, mixed with the growing fear in the pit of Margit's stomach, made her dizzy. Where was Lilly? Where could she have gone? She could not have disappeared in the middle of the night, and it was unthinkable that she could have left the apartment on her own. Margit was frantic, turning her head in all directions as if Lilly might magically appear in a corner of the room. And then Margit froze once more. There was that sound again, a dull scraping and then a small thump. And all at once Margit realized that the noise was coming from inside the small closet in the living room.

Cautiously, Margit crept toward the closet door. She turned the handle slowly, pulled the door open a crack, and peered inside. At first she couldn't see a thing. It was pitch-black. She pulled the door open more fully, allowing the grey light from the living room to illuminate the inside of the closet. And there was Lilly, curled up in a ball on the floor, her head on a pillow and a blanket draped over her small body. Margit gasped, and at that same moment Lilly woke up.

Margit wasn't sure what it was that made Lilly cry out. But she could only imagine how terrifying it must have been for Lilly to be awakened by Margit's shadowy figure towering over her. In the darkness, Margit must have looked like a dark giant, an oversized monster hovering over Lilly and reaching out for her. And when Lilly screamed, the sound was chilling, a long hair-raising cry that echoed throughout the apartment. Within seconds, Mamma and Papa had come running into the living room to join Margit.

"What happened?" Mamma exclaimed. She knelt down and scooped Lilly out of the closet and into her arms, fighting to comfort the terrified child. Lilly was still shrieking, throwing her head back and pounding her fists into Mamma's chest. Papa flicked on the living-room light and fumbled with his glasses.

"I don't know," Margit said. She had to raise her voice to be heard above Lilly's screams. "I heard a noise in the living room, and when

I came out here, Lilly was gone. I looked everywhere and then I found her here in the closet.
When she heard me open the door, she just
started screaming."

"Shhhh, Lilly," Mamma soothed. "*Nic wam tu
nie grozi.* You're safe here. Shhhh …" Mamma
rocked Lilly back and forth until Lilly's screams
turned to cries, and then to soft whimpers.

Margit was still shaken. Papa placed his arm
protectively around his daughter. "Come,
Margitka," Papa said. "Mamma will put Lilly to
bed and we'll make some tea." Gently, he guided
his daughter into the kitchen and seated her at
the table while he put a kettle of water on the
stove to boil. Mamma joined them several
minutes later.

"She's sleeping again, poor child. And this time
in her bed." Mamma slumped heavily in a chair
and gratefully accepted tea from Papa.

"Mamma, I don't understand what's going on,"
Margit cried. "What was Lilly doing sleeping in
the closet, on the floor?" Margit shook her head.

This situation with Lilly was becoming stranger by the minute.

Mamma sighed and rested her head on her arm as she gazed at her daughter. Her eyes were heavy and she too seemed at a loss. "I'm not sure I understand everything, Margitka. There's still so much we don't know about Lilly's past."

"We do know that it was very dangerous for her to be hiding with her neighbour," continued Papa. "There were frequent raids on her town by soldiers looking for Jews who might have been left behind. If Lilly had been discovered, she would have been arrested, and her neighbour would have been punished. Helping a Jewish person was against the law."

He continued, looking thoughtful. "The neighbour might have hidden her in a closet, thinking it would be safer there. I imagine there were many times Lilly slept on a hard closet floor, scared that the soldiers might arrive at any moment. It must have terrified her when you opened the door to the closet in the middle of the night."

Margit sat back in her chair, then said, "She thought I was a soldier coming to arrest her." Things were beginning to make more sense— Lilly's silence, the fear in her eyes. "No wonder she screamed when I opened the door."

Mamma nodded. "Lilly doesn't yet accept that the dangers have passed, that she doesn't need to hide anymore. That will take time. Remember, Margit —"

"I know what you're going to say," interrupted Margit. "I have to be patient."

Papa smiled and rubbed his eyes. "We all do."

CHAPTER N.º 5

Papa's alarm clock rang loudly the next morning, echoing through the apartment and pounding into Margit's head. Margit groaned and rolled over in bed. She was exhausted after her sleepless night. But at the same time, she was eager to see Lilly. She dragged herself out of bed and stumbled into the living room. Lilly was up and dressed, seated quietly in a chair. Next to her, the bed had been folded back into a couch. There was no evidence of the previous night's commotion. Lilly was silent, as usual. But Margit sensed something slightly different. Was it her imagination, or did Lilly look calmer, more peaceful and relaxed?

"Good morning," said Margit. There was a long pause. Margit waited. *Say something,* she silently prayed. *Just try to talk to me. I'm not going to hurt you.*

Lilly stared for the longest time, and Margit sighed. She was just about to turn away, when Lilly leaned forward, opened her mouth, and spoke in a small but clear voice. "Good … morning," she said, and then sat back in her chair.

Margit's mouth dropped open. Lilly had spoken. She had responded to Margit. It was just a tiny step forward, but it was something. "You talked!" cried Margit. "That's great! I mean, good morning! Good morning!"

"Good morning," Lilly replied again, this time with a small smile.

Margit grinned and bounced up and down. "Mamma," she yelled. "Come here! Lilly talked!"

Mamma appeared from the kitchen with Jack close behind. "That's wonderful, Margit. You see? Things are changing already."

"Good morning," said Lilly to Jack. Jack giggled and ran over to Lilly, throwing himself onto her lap.

"Dibby talk," he shouted. Lilly smiled and stroked Jack's head.

Margit watched with new hope and excitement. Maybe the incident the previous night had triggered something for Lilly. Maybe she was beginning to realize that this family was here to help her, not to harm her. It was too much to wish for, but Margit hoped that this was a turning point for Lilly and for all of them.

"And now you must get dressed quickly, and come and eat breakfast," Mamma said. "In all the excitement I forgot to tell you that a reporter from the *Telegram* newspaper is coming over this morning. The Jewish orphans that have come to Toronto are getting some attention. The reporter wants to take a picture of Lilly and the whole family for his paper."

Margit's eyes shone brightly. Finally it felt again as if there were things to look forward to. Margit dressed and quickly ate her breakfast. Then she helped Mamma tidy the apartment, all the while pointing things out to Lilly.

"This is a bed," she said, "and a chair."

"Bed," Lilly repeated. "Chair."

Slowly but surely, Lilly added English words to her collection. "Book, table, lamp, doll." Lilly would repeat the words slowly and then point to something else as the lesson continued. Sometimes Lilly's eyes would cloud over and she would retreat, back into that silent, distant world of hers. "This is a window," Margit said at one point, and waited for a response. But Lilly only stared and said nothing. Margit knew that there was still a long way to go before Lilly would fully relax. Learning English would help, but that was only one part of it. Coming to terms with her deep fears would be an even more important part of Lilly's progress.

The doorbell rang just as Margit was beginning to name the parts of the body, using Jack as a model. Jack roared with laughter every time Margit touched his nose, his chin, and his tummy.

"I'll get it," Margit shouted, running to the apartment door and straightening her blouse before she reached over to open it. But it wasn't the reporter standing there. It was Alice.

"Oh, hi," Margit said, looking over Alice's shoulder. "I was expecting someone else."

"I can see that." Alice waited a moment. "Is it okay if I come in? I thought we could take Lilly out for a walk."

Margit shook her head and explained about the reporter. "I don't think you should stay," she added.

Alice frowned. "You know, Margit, I haven't seen you in days, not since Lilly arrived. You haven't come to the market, you won't go to the park with me, and you don't answer the telephone when I call. I know you need to spend time with Lilly, but what about me?"

Margit's cheeks flamed and a wave of anger swept over her. Couldn't Alice see that there were important things going on? "I'm busy right now, Alice. Lilly needs me. She's just starting to talk and I have to be here for her. Don't you understand that?"

"I understand that I'm your friend too. I hope you haven't forgotten that." With that, Alice turned and walked down the stairs.

Margit stared after her. This was so unfair. Alice was being selfish and mean. It was true that Margit had not really seen Alice in some time, had not even tried to meet up with her or to call her. But surely Alice could understand why. It wasn't that Margit was rejecting Alice. It was just that for the time being, Lilly was more important.

Margit shook her head and closed the door. She didn't want to think about this right now. She was just beginning to connect with Lilly, and she didn't want anything to spoil this moment. In any case, there was no time to dwell on these thoughts, because moments later the doorbell rang again. This time it was the reporter standing there.

"Hello, young lady," the man said when Margit opened the door for a second time. "The name's Tom Simpson. I'm with the *Toronto Telegram*. Is this where the Freed family lives?"

Mr. Simpson was a tall, gangly-looking man, with a funny hat perched on the back of his head and glasses sliding partway down his nose. He peered over the glasses at Margit, and then slung his camera over his shoulder as Margit invited him inside.

"Just one picture, and I'll be out of your hair," he explained to Margit and her family. Margit, noting the puzzled looks on the faces of her parents, did a quick translation. Though their English was quite good, some expressions were still confusing for them.

Mr. Simpson lined the family up for their photograph. Mamma and Papa stood in the back, with Margit and Lilly next to one another in front of them. Jack was placed right in the front. Lilly placed her hand on Jack's shoulder, but Jack didn't need any supervision. He loved pictures and happily smiled for the photographer.

"I'll take a couple more just to be on the safe side," said Mr. Simpson. "You young orphans are getting a lot of attention these days, eh? There are lots of pictures and stories in all the papers about the bunch of you that have come to live in Canada." Lilly had been part of a group of more than one thousand Jewish orphans who had been brought to Canada after the war. The Canadian Jewish Congress had arranged the whole thing, and had found the families like Margit's who would adopt these children.

Lilly shrank back when the reporter began to speak. Perhaps there was something about his tall frame that frightened her. "Lilly doesn't speak any English," Margit explained. "I think she's a little nervous around strangers."

"Don't worry, miss," Mr. Simpson said, shrugging his shoulders. "I'll tell you what I'm going

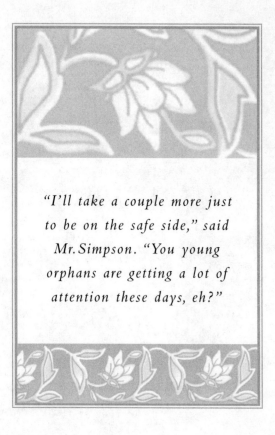

"I'll take a couple more just to be on the safe side," said Mr. Simpson. "You young orphans are getting a lot of attention these days, eh?"

to do. When I have these pictures developed, I'll drop a copy by for your family. How's that? You'll have your very own souvenir—a picture of your new family."

Lilly moved back even farther. Margit could see that scared look in her eyes, like a deer out in an open field that was desperately looking for cover. Margit turned to her parents for help. Papa knew what to do at once.

"We thank you for today," Papa said in his broken English. "And we look forward to the picture." With that, Papa shook hands with Mr. Simpson, quickly guided him to the door, and ushered him out.

CHAPTER N.º 6

*That morning had been a small break-*through for Lilly, and over the next weeks, slowly but surely, she began to talk more. She became more curious about English words, and even started asking a few questions. Margit, for her part, was more determined than ever to work at their friendship. Sometimes the conversations with Lilly were stiff and formal.

"How are you feeling?" Margit would ask.

"Fine," Lilly would reply.

"Would you like anything?"

"No, thank you."

Other times, Margit felt as if they were making real progress together. Margit took Lilly everywhere—to the playground, the synagogue, the market stores, and into neighbouring streets. Margit pointed out new things to Lilly, and slowly and patiently talked to her about life in the neighbourhood.

"This is where you will go to school in September," Margit said one day as they walked together on the street.

"I like school," Lilly said. "I like to read books."

Margit felt her chest bursting with excitement. "It may be hard for you at first, but I'll be there to help," Margit offered.

"I miss my—" Lilly stopped and became silent once more. Margit watched and said nothing. One of the things she had learned was that if Lilly was pushed, she became quieter and more withdrawn. It was a pattern that was still very frustrating for Margit. Margit was thrilled that Lilly was beginning to open up, but still, something was missing. There was a wall between them that you couldn't see, as solid and impassable as any physical structure. Lilly would not let Margit in to her private thoughts and deep feelings.

"Why isn't Lilly more friendly?" Margit complained to Mamma day after day. "Why isn't she happier here? She talks to me now, but I don't feel like I'm really getting close to her."

And Mamma's answer was always the same. "Be patient, Margitka. It will all come in time. You can't make Lilly get close to you. She has to do that on her own."

Margit sighed and shook her head. She longed to sit down with Lilly and have a real conversation with her—the kind where you talked about everything, where you shared your deepest secrets and your most important dreams. She longed for Lilly to be a real friend, and it wasn't happening fast enough.

One day, a few weeks later, Mamma sent Lilly and Margit to the market. "I need some milk and some eggs, Margit. Take Lilly and I'll look after

Jack here at home, so the two of you can have some time together."

Margit nodded and headed out the door with Lilly. Spending private time with Lilly away from Jack was a treat. When Jack was there, he occupied all of Lilly's attention. Even though they said little to one another, Margit had the feeling that Lilly was closest to Jack of anyone in her family. It made Margit envious.

It was another hot summer day. The heat was so thick you could practically see it rising from the pavement. And the market was full of shoppers, jostling against one another on the sidewalk and pushing up against the small shops that dotted the neighbourhood. Margit paused in front of a small stand where a vendor was selling fresh orange juice and lemonade. One by one, he placed freshly cut fruit onto a silver strainer and squeezed down on the handle. Juice trickled out into a large container half-buried in a bucket of ice. Bees buzzed overhead, attracted to the sticky sweetness. The smell of freshly squeezed juice floated through the air.

"Would you like something to drink, Lilly?" Margit asked.

"Yes, please. Some juice, please," Lilly answered.

"The first time I came to the market, I got into trouble because the owner of one of the stores thought that I had stolen something from his stall. That's when I met Alice. She came to help me. I didn't steal of course, but the shopkeeper thought ..." Margit stopped talking when she realized that Lilly wasn't listening. Lilly had turned her back, seemingly not interested in the conversation.

Margit brushed her curls off of her forehead and frowned. Lilly always seemed to turn away just when Margit was about to say something personal. Margit heaved a sigh. *I can't make Lilly get close to me*, she thought, echoing Mamma's wise words. Margit had just finished paying for two small glasses of orange juice when suddenly she spied Alice in the distance. Alice was walking with Janet, a girl who went to school with them. The two girls were deep in conversation.

"Alice!" Margit was delighted to see her friend, and eager to talk to her. "Alice!" Margit called again. She waved her arms in the air.

Alice looked up briefly, and then turned back to her conversation with Janet.

That's funny, thought Margit. *I wonder why she doesn't answer me. Maybe she didn't hear me, or didn't see me.* Margit quickly finished her juice, grabbed Lilly by the arm, and walked over to where Alice was standing.

"Hi, Alice," Margit said when she reached her friend. Alice looked up blankly. "I haven't seen you in ages," Margit continued. "What have you been doing? Are you working in your parents' store? Do you want to come over? Do you want to go to a movie? I've got so much to talk to you about!" Margit knew that she was babbling, but she couldn't help it. All the conversation had been bottled up inside of her for too long. Seeing Alice reminded Margit of how wonderful it was to have a friend to talk to. She had missed Alice, and hadn't realized how much until this moment.

Alice stared at Margit—a long, hard gaze that seemed to pierce right through her. When Alice finally spoke, her voice was cool and unemotional. "I guess you've been busy with too many other important things," she said.

"What do you mean?" Margit said in a small voice. "I'm not too busy for you, Alice."

"That's not what you said a few weeks ago. When you said you couldn't spend time with me, I decided to see some of my other friends. Janet and I have been doing all kinds of things together—movies, shopping, going to the park."

Margit eyed Janet enviously. "But, maybe I could come along," Margit said.

Alice shook her head. "I don't think so. We've got too many plans. You understand, don't you?" With that, Alice turned her back, linked arms with Janet, and walked away, leaving Margit standing alone with Lilly next to her.

Margit's mind was spinning, and she felt as if her world was collapsing around her. She could not believe what had just happened. Here she was, trying desperately to build a friendship with Lilly, something that was just barely working. But by spending all of her time with Lilly, she had completely deserted Alice. Now Margit felt as if she had no one to call her "friend." She had ruined everything.

Margit felt hot tears rise in her eyes, and she quickly brushed them away before Lilly could see anything. Lilly stared at Margit's face. Lilly must have sensed the coldness in Alice's voice, even if she didn't understand all of the conversation.

"Come on, Lilly," Margit said, her voice trembling. "I need to go home."

Margit burst through the door of her apartment with Lilly close behind. Neither of the two girls had said anything on the walk home from the market. Lilly must have sensed Margit's despair, and at one point she had even reached up to take Margit's hand. But Margit barely noticed. She had to get home. She had to talk to Mamma. Mamma would help her sort everything out— she would figure out what Margit needed to do to get Alice back. Margit would apologize to Alice, make her a card, or go to her house. Whatever it took, Margit would do it. Her friendship with Alice meant the world to Margit, and she was determined to work this out.

Mamma took one look at Margit's face and steered her into the kitchen. Lilly retreated to the couch in the living room, where she perched herself uneasily in one corner. "Sit down, Margit," Mamma said as Margit began to blurt out everything that had happened at the market. The story was coming out of Margit in a jumbled mess of thoughts and half-sentences. "Catch your breath and tell me slowly what happened," Mamma said.

Margit slumped heavily on the chair in the kitchen.

"I didn't meant to hurt Alice," moaned Margit as she finished telling the story once more. "I just needed to spend more time with Lilly. But now I feel as if I don't have any friends left at all." Margit buried her face in her hands. She had made a mess of everything.

Mamma sat down next to her daughter and placed a loving hand on her arm. "I'm so sorry, my darling. This has been a difficult time for you, hasn't it? But these are things that can be fixed," Mamma said. "I know how important Alice is to you. And I'm certain Alice knows this too. Right now she must be feeling hurt and left out. It's not so different from how you have been feeling with Lilly."

Margit lifted her head, startled by this.

"You have been feeling as if Lilly doesn't care about you, doesn't want to be your friend," Mamma continued. "Well, isn't that the same feeling that Alice has right now? She has been trying to see you and spend time with you, but you've turned her away."

"But—" Margit began to protest.

"Yes, yes, I know. It's because you have to spend time with Lilly. Think about how that feels to Alice."

Margit sat back in her seat and slowly began to nod her head. Mamma was right. Margit had done to Alice exactly what she felt Lilly was doing to her. "But what am I going to do?" Margit wailed.

Mamma sighed. "You'll be patient, as you've been with Lilly. You'll find a way to repair your friendship with Alice. It's too important to you."

Of course it was important, Margit thought. But how was she going to fix it? Mamma rose from the kitchen table, leaving Margit alone to think. She had to do something, and she had to do it quickly. She had to go back to the market and find Alice. That was the first thing she was going to do. She couldn't let this wait another minute. Margit wasn't at all sure of what she would say to Alice once she found her, but somehow, when the time came, she would find the right words.

Margit nodded her head with new determination and was just about to push away from the table when she heard the scream coming from the living room. The second Margit heard the sound, she knew that it was Lilly. It was the same desperate, terrifying wail that Margit had heard the night she found Lilly sleeping in the closet.

Margit charged out into the living room with Mamma at her heels. Lilly was standing in the middle of the room, frantically turning her head this way and that, searching for something.

"What happened?" Margit cried. "Lilly, what's wrong?"

Lilly didn't answer. Her body jolted and twisted. One minute she was diving onto the floor, searching under the sofa. The next minute she was inside the closet, pulling things out and dropping them onto the floor.

"Lilly!" Margit repeated. Finally, Lilly turned to face Margit and her mother. "What's wrong?" Margit demanded again.

"My picture," Lilly finally replied in a small breathless voice. "My picture."

Lilly's precious photograph of her parents was gone. She had left it next to the sofa as she always did, but when she returned from the market with Margit it was nowhere to be found.

Margit spent the next few minutes searching the living room. She rummaged through the closet, lifted every cushion off the sofa, searched behind the chairs, and combed through the books on the bookshelf. But she found nothing. Mamma sat with Lilly, holding her and stroking her head while Margit searched. And all the while, Lilly whimpered sadly like an injured animal lost in the forest. "My photo," she wept. "*Mamusia*, Papa, my photo."

It was heartbreaking to listen to. Margit continued to search, scouring every corner of the living room. Still, she could not find the picture. *This was impossible*, Margit thought in desperation. The picture could not have disappeared into thin air. But there was no sign of it. Margit was on the verge of giving up when she heard a soft rustle and a giggle coming from her own bedroom on the other side of the curtain.

"Mamma," said Margit. "Where's Jack?"

Mamma looked up. "I left him napping in my bedroom, but ..."

Mamma's eyes locked with Margit's, and it was as if a single realization flashed between them.

Margit stood up from the floor where she had been searching, walked toward her curtain, pulled it aside, and peered around the corner. There was Jack seated on Margit's bed. He held Lilly's picture in one hand and a red coloured crayon in the other. It did not take Margit long to see that Jack had taken the coloured crayon and drawn all over Lilly's family photo.

This isn't happening, Margit prayed as she quietly approached the bed. Then out loud, "Jack!" she said hoarsely.

At the sound of Margit's voice, Jack looked up from his work. His face broke into a happy grin when he saw his sister standing above him. "A picture, Mah-git," Jack said, happily holding up the photo.

"Oh no," Margit groaned. "Jack, what have you done?"

"I draw," Jack said, bending over to continue with his artwork.

"No," Margit cried, grabbing the crayon out of Jack's hand. But it was too late. Margit could not believe what she was staring at. With his bright red crayon, Jack had drawn a big red circle around the face of Lilly's mother. He had painted her lips bright red and had done the same with the face of Lilly's father. Jack had ruined the picture.

Margit stood there, staring in horror at the photograph while Jack reached up trying to reclaim it. Neither Jack nor Margit noticed that Lilly had walked over to the curtain and around it into Margit's bedroom. When Margit heard the gasp behind her, she spun around to face Lilly.

Lilly stared at the photo, her face drained of colour and her eyes wide as two moons.

"Hi, Dibby," said Jack when he saw Lilly standing at the entrance to Margit's bedroom. "I draw."

"My photo," Lilly screamed. "Look at my photo!" She pounced on the picture, tearing it from Margit's hands and burying her face in the picture. "My photo." She repeated the words over and over, while she rocked back and forth clutching the picture.

Mamma was there in a second.

It took hours to calm Lilly. She sobbed and cried and shouted—a combination of her native Polish and her broken English. "My photo, *moje zdjęcie, moja rodzina,* my family!"

Jack was equally inconsolable. "I sorry, Dibby," he wailed. "I so sorry!" How could Jack possibly have understood that by drawing on Lilly's photo, he had ruined her one and only keepsake from her parents? He had thought he was making her a present, something that would make her laugh. He could not have been more wrong.

It took hours to calm Lilly.
She sobbed and cried
and shouted ...

When Papa arrived home from work, the apartment was in chaos. Lilly was sobbing uncontrollably on the sofa, Jack was screaming from the bedroom, and Mamma and Margit were running between the two of them, trying unsuccessfully to calm the situation.

"Please try to understand," Margit begged of Lilly. "Jack didn't mean it. He thought he was making something that you would like." Lilly wailed some more and didn't answer.

"Jack, you know better than to touch things that don't belong to you," Margit scolded Jack.

"I make a picture for Dibby!" Jack screamed.

Margit was desperate to help calm the situation. In the meantime, any thoughts of seeing Alice evaporated. Alice would have to wait while Margit's family was sorting out this mess at home.

Mamma was the one who finally managed to get Lilly and Jack settled and sleeping. Jack cried himself to sleep, still sobbing Lilly's name. Lilly, meanwhile, became quiet and withdrawn, pulling back into that protective shell of hers and shutting everyone out. Margit felt so bad for both of them. Jack really didn't know any better. After all, he was still so little, and he thought he was doing something special for Lilly. But for Lilly, the destruction of her precious photograph must have felt like the loss of her parents all over again.

Margit worried about her little brother and Lilly, and wondered how this was ever going to be resolved. And on top of all of this, Margit worried about herself and her rocky friendship with Alice. She needed to talk to Alice as soon as she could. And right now, Margit had no idea when that might be.

By the time Margit finally laid her head on her own pillow, she was so exhausted from the commotion and the worrying that within just minutes she had fallen into a deep sleep.

It was still early when Margit awoke the next day. The first morning rays of the rising sun were just beginning to filter into the apartment. Margit could hear the milk truck motoring past the open window, squealing to a stop at every other house, followed by the clinking of glass as the milkman collected the empties and left full bottles in their place. But mostly it was peaceful in the apartment, and Margit closed her eyes a little longer, trying to savour the quiet and calm of this early morning. No one was awake yet in the apartment, but it wouldn't be long before Margit would hear Mamma's footsteps heading for the kitchen to begin making tea and preparing breakfast. Papa would follow shortly after that, and then Margit knew she would hear their soft voices as they whispered a conversation reserved only for each other. When Jack awoke, the peacefulness of the morning would evaporate. That was usually Margit's cue to get up. Papa always joked that Jack had replaced the alarm clock in Margit's life.

But this morning was different, and Margit was already wide awake. Her mind was still racing from the chaotic events of the previous night. Jack would be fine, Margit knew. In a day or two, he would forget what he had done to Lilly's picture—it was so easy for a little boy his age to move on with things. But how was Lilly ever going to recover from the destruction of her family photo? And how was Margit ever going to repair her friendship with Alice? These thoughts and questions swirled about in Margit's head until she finally pushed the covers aside and got out of bed. *Might as well get up and help Mamma,* she thought.

The floor felt cool under Margit's feet in contrast to the heat that was already settling inside the apartment. Margit walked softly across her bedroom. She took a deep breath before pushing the curtain aside and entering the living room. She had the speech already prepared in her mind, the comforting words she would offer to Lilly by way of apology for the previous night.

"We're here for you, Lilly," she would say. "We want to be your family now. I know it's not the same as your real family, but please give us a chance." Would Lilly listen? Would she understand that Margit and her parents, and even Jack, were trying their hardest to love Lilly and be her friend? Margit would not know the answer to these questions. When she rounded the corner of her bedroom and saw the couch already neatly made up and the empty closet next to it, she knew instantly that Lilly had run away.

For a brief second Margit froze while new thoughts and fears invaded her mind. But a moment later, she was pounding on her parents' bedroom door.

"Mamma, Papa!" Margit cried urgently. "Get up, quickly! Lilly's gone. I think she's run away!"

Margit had barely finished the sentence when Mamma flung open the bedroom door. Papa was right behind her.

"She's gone," Margit repeated. "She's taken her suitcase and left."

Papa sprinted for the apartment door and opened it wide, peering down the stairs, hoping beyond hope that Lilly might still be there. Mamma scoured inside the closet. Perhaps Lilly had left something behind—a letter or another clue to her whereabouts. There was nothing.

"We must call the police," Papa said, locking eyes with Mamma. She nodded.

Margit froze. The last time she had talked with a police officer was the time Jack had disappeared in the Eaton's department store. He had wandered away one day when he was out with Margit and Alice. The girls, who were watching him, had turned away for just a moment. That was when he had disappeared. Luckily, he had been found a short time later, sleeping peacefully underneath a display counter. Margit did not think the situation with Lilly would resolve itself so easily.

"We need to call the Jewish Congress as well," added Mamma. "They need to know that Lilly is missing."

Papa nodded. He was already talking to the police on the telephone, slowly explaining what had happened. "Yes, a little girl," he said. "She is nine years old. Please hurry," he added. "She is all alone, and she only speaks a little English."

The police were there in a matter of minutes, followed closely by a lady from the Toronto branch of the Canadian Jewish Congress.

"She is not the first of our children to run away," Mrs. Wolfe explained gently to Margit's family. "Many of these children have settled easily into our country. But many have had a difficult adjustment. They miss their homes so much. And they are still coping with the loss of their own families, not to mention trauma of their own."

That sounds just like Lilly, thought Margit.

"Is there anything you can think of that might have triggered this?" asked the man from the police. Police Officer Harrison was taking notes while the grown-ups talked. "Anything," he added, "that the little girl might have said— anything at all."

Margit gulped and stared guiltily at her parents. Mamma quickly explained about the picture and Jack's uninvited drawing. The police officer nodded and jotted something down in his notebook.

"You mustn't feel responsible for this," Mrs. Wolfe added, approaching Margit and reaching down to take her hand. "We will find Lilly. I promise."

CHAPTER N.º 9

After Police Officer Harrison and Mrs. Wolfe left, Margit paced impatiently around the apartment. "When are they going to let us know something?" she asked moments later.

"Margit, they have just left here," replied Papa. "The police will need to begin searching for Lilly—going to all of the places you have been with her. It will take time." Papa was trying to reassure Margit, but it didn't work.

"But they did say they would call as soon as they knew anything, didn't they, Papa?" Margit asked. "Didn't Mrs. Wolfe say she would call just to keep us posted?" Margit continued to pace around the apartment.

"Margit, you will just have to be patient," said Mamma wearily.

There was that word, "patient," again. How could Margit be patient when Lilly was wandering lost somewhere on the streets of Toronto? How could Margit be calm when Lilly might be hurt or scared? Besides, it didn't help Margit that Mamma and Papa looked just as worried as Margit herself was feeling.

Margit could see the fear in their faces. As much as they reassured her and told her that everything would be fine, Margit sensed their uncertainty. And that scared her even more. Whenever Margit worried about anything, she relied on her parents' strength and certainty to take her own fears away. Their confidence had always given Margit courage. But now Mamma looked pale. Papa was trying to be strong, but he too was quiet, and sat weakly in the big armchair, holding his head and saying little.

Margit knew that she had to do something. She couldn't just sit at home and wait, not knowing when or if the police would contact her family. And in that moment, Margit realized exactly what she had to do. Margit had to see Alice. Alice would know what to do. She would have some idea of where to look for Lilly. Alice would help—unless, that is, she was still too angry with Margit to help. Margit gulped and shook her head. She couldn't worry about that right now. She needed to go to Alice's house and explain the whole situation.

"I can't sit around here anymore," Margit announced to her parents as she headed out the door toward Alice's home. "I'm going out for a walk."

Alice's mother answered the door when Margit rang the bell. "Oh, hello, dear," Mrs. Donald said. "I'll call Alice, but I'm not sure that she will come to the door. I'm so upset that the two of you have been quarrelling." She smiled sympathetically at Margit.

"Please, Mrs. Donald," begged Margit. "I have to see her."

Mrs. Donald nodded and invited Margit inside. She turned and disappeared into another room while Margit waited at the door. A moment later, Alice appeared in front of Margit.

"Alice!" cried Margit when she saw her friend. "I'm so glad to see you. I need your help."

A long silent moment passed while Alice eyed Margit. When Alice finally spoke, her voice was tight and cool. "Where's your new best friend?" she asked, peering around Margit to the front door. "Isn't Lilly the one you want?"

"Lilly's run away," blurted Margit. "I woke up this morning and she was gone." Quickly Margit went on to explain about Lilly's photograph and Jack's unfortunate drawing. "The police are looking for Lilly right now, but I can't stand waiting for them to call us. Please, Alice," Margit begged. "Please help me. Together I know we can find Lilly. And besides," Margit added quietly, "*you're* my best friend."

Margit paused. Alice stared back at her, frowning. And then Alice took a deep breath and began to talk.

"I was so angry with you, Margit," said Alice. "You took advantage of our friendship. You hurt me."

Margit nodded. "I know. I know, and I'm so sorry. I can't believe I deserted you. I can't believe I pushed you away."

"You say I'm your best friend, but that's not the way friends treat each other."

"You're right," agreed Margit. "I was wrong to ignore you. I don't know why I didn't see that, Alice. I was just so caught up in trying to be Lilly's friend that I forgot how important you are to me. And now I'm so afraid that I've lost you both." Margit whispered the last words and lowered her head. She felt the tears welling behind her eyes and she blinked quickly. But when she looked up, Alice's face had softened.

"You can't get rid of me that easily," Alice finally said.

"Are we still friends?" asked Margit.

There was a brief pause, and then Alice smiled. "Of course we're friends. But," she added, "don't ever do anything like that to me again."

Margit grinned and grabbed her friend for a tight hug. "I missed you so much, Alice."

"Me too," said Alice, returning the hug.

"Will you help me find Lilly?" Margit asked, staring into Alice's eyes.

Alice nodded. "Let's start looking."

CHAPTER Nº 10

"*Okay,*" *said Alice as the two girls* dashed out the door and onto the streets of Toronto. "Think back to all of the places that you've been with Lilly—every store, every street."

Margit paused and turned to face Alice. "We've gone to so many places. I don't even know where to begin." She and Lilly had walked on countless streets. They had gone into so many parks, walked into dozens of stores, ridden the streetcars and the buses. How could she retrace the many steps the two of them had taken?

Alice nodded understandingly. "Then let's start with the major places first. Let's go to the market."

Alice and Margit crossed over Spadina Avenue and entered the market at Baldwin Street. Together, they walked the small narrow streets of the market, pausing to go inside each and every store that Margit could remember going into with Lilly. Like two young detectives, Margit and Alice questioned the shopkeepers and vendors.

"Have you seen a little girl in your store today?" Alice would ask.

"She is nine years old and has straight brown hair," Margit would add. "She's got sad eyes and doesn't smile very much."

One after another, the shopkeepers would stroke their chins thoughtfully and then shake their heads. No one matching Lilly's description had been seen that day.

At one point Margit stopped to call home, using the telephone in the Donalds' flower shop. "Have the police called yet?" Margit asked when her father answered. Margit listened and then shook her head in response to Alice's silent question. There was still no word from the police about Lilly's whereabouts.

After leaving the market, Alice and Margit headed for their school. They walked the perimeter of the playground, stopping everyone they saw and giving them Lilly's description. From there, the girls headed for the park, retracing the routes Margit had taken and asking strangers about Lilly. Margit and Alice asked the same series of questions of every person they stopped, and the answer was always the same: no one had seen Lilly.

On the outside Margit appeared calm. But inside, her stomach was twisted with fear, and her mind raced with unimaginable thoughts and visions. She pictured Lilly, all alone in some forgotten alleyway. She could see her approaching strangers, asking for help and being ignored because no one could understand her. Margit's mind even raced to images of Lilly hidden in a closet somewhere, crying out for her parents and terrified of every footstep that approached. Margit felt helpless and desperate as the minutes ticked by with no sign of Lilly.

After combing the streets of Toronto for several hours, Alice and Margit finally collapsed in exhaustion onto a small bench beneath a big, shady elm tree. The leaves provided welcome shelter from the sun's persistent heat, and Margit closed her eyes, trying to catch a bit of the breeze as it drifted by. "What do we do now?" she asked.

"I guess we move on," replied Alice. "Let's go to some other parks, and then maybe the department store, and then—"

"I just feel like this isn't working," interrupted Margit. "I don't think we're going to find Lilly in any of those places." Try as she might, Margit could not imagine that she and Alice would suddenly run into Lilly in one of the many places she had visited with Lilly in the past. As hard as it was to believe, it appeared that Lilly had truly vanished.

"Maybe we need to do this differently," said Alice suddenly. "Maybe we need to stop looking for Lilly and start thinking like Lilly."

Margit looked up. What could Alice possibly mean by that?

"You said that Lilly was really upset with Jack's drawing," continued Alice.

"It was terrible, Alice," Margit answered. "It was like Jack had destroyed her family."

"Okay, so she ran away because she was angry, and she was thinking about her real family— maybe even wanting to be with them." Alice's hand traced an imaginary line on the bench between the two girls. It was as if she were mapping out Lilly's route.

"But that's just it," replied Margit, turning away from Alice. This situation was becoming more and more confusing. Where was Alice going with all of this? "Lilly doesn't have any family," she said. "*We're* supposed to be her family, but she doesn't seem to want us anymore. And who can blame her after what Jack did?

Right now, I don't think she likes anything about being here in Canada."

Alice sat straight up. "If she doesn't like being in Canada, then where would she want to go?"

Margit shrugged her shoulders. "Probably back to her home, but that's impossible too."

Alice grabbed Margit's arm as if the pieces of the puzzle had suddenly come together for her. "But if she *were* trying to get back home, then there's only one place she could have gone."

Margit turned to face Alice, and suddenly the answer was there. "The train station." As soon as the words were out of her mouth, the situation was clear. It was as if a light bulb had gone on in Margit's mind. Lilly was trying to get home, trying to get on a train to Halifax and then maybe even on a boat back to Europe. As crazy as it seemed, Margit knew with certainty that Lilly must have gone to the train station. Why had Margit not thought of it earlier? In the confusion of Lilly's disappearance, she had thought only of the immediate past, the places where she and Lilly had gone in the preceding weeks. But if Lilly were really trying to run away, then it made sense that she would be trying to run to a place where her life had begun, and where her family had once lived. "Alice, you're brilliant," said Margit, hugging her friend. "We've got to get to the train station."

CHAPTER N° 11

Margit and Alice pushed open the heavy glass doors and entered into the large central hall of Union Station.

"What will you say to Lilly when you see her?" Alice had asked during the seemingly endless journey down Spadina Avenue and across Front Street.

That question spun around in Margit's head along with so many others. Would Lilly talk? Would she be angry? Would she run away again? And most of all, would she agree to return with Margit to her home?

Margit and Alice looked around the crowded hall. The station was packed with busy travellers arriving from and departing for places across the country. A porter wheeled a heavy cart past Alice and Margit. The cart was piled high with multicoloured suitcases in every imaginable shape and size. Two children followed, laughing and running around the enormous limestone columns that dotted the station. Their parents called out to them to behave and walk slowly. Alice pointed in the direction of one of the ticket counters. "Let's ask about the trains to Halifax."

Margit nodded, and the two girls ran across the hall. Their feet clattered on the shiny marble floors and echoed up to the high vaulted ceiling. There was a long line leading up to the ticket counter, and Margit and Alice waited impatiently for the line to move. "Excuse me," Margit asked when she and Alice finally made it to the front. "Would you please tell me when the next train for Halifax is leaving?"

The young woman behind the desk opened a large logbook in front of her and scanned down the column of departures. "Let's see," she said. "There is a train leaving in thirty minutes. It will be boarding shortly. People are lining up on plat-form D down the hallway and to the left. Would you like to buy a—"

"Thank you!" Margit did not wait to hear the end of the woman's question. She grabbed Alice by the arm and manoeuvred her down the hallway toward the departure platforms. There were crowds already forming in front of several doors as travel-lers lined up for their trains. The train to Halifax would be boarding in a few minutes, and Margit and Alice only had a short time to find Lilly and figure out what they were going to do with her.

"There's platform D," said Alice, pointing toward a large sign that hung from the ceiling.

"But where's Lilly?" Margit asked anxiously. At least fifty people were lined up under the sign. Margit scanned the crowd, her eyes moving quickly across the crowd of men, women, and children, all jostling to get to the front and board the train. And just then, as if someone had heard her question, the crowd shifted and parted, and there was Lilly. She was near the front of the line, standing next to an official from the station. He was holding Lilly's hand tightly. Her face was lowered as she stood obediently and silently. She looked tiny and lost in the milling crowd.

"Lilly!" Margit called out and waved her arms above her head.

At the sound of her name, Lilly looked up. Even from a distance, Margit could see that Lilly had been crying. Her eyes were puffy and red. Her cheeks were smudged with the remains of tears, and she sniffled slightly and sucked in a small gulp of air. Her small suitcase sat on the ground next to her. In her free hand, she still clutched the photo of her family, its red-crayoned circles beaming out across the hallway at Margit.

When Margit and Alice reached Lilly, Margit grabbed her in a tight hug. "Oh, Lilly," she whispered. "I'm so glad we found you." Lilly's free arm rested limply at her side, and she did not respond.

"Is she with you?" the uniformed official asked. "I caught this little one trying to sneak on board the train here. I was just waiting for all the folks to board, and then I was going to call the police." The man continued to hold on to Lilly's hand as he addressed Margit and Alice.

"Yes," replied Margit. "She's with us. She's my … my sister." Lilly looked up, startled, and stared at Margit. Margit went on to explain that Lilly had run away from home that morning, and that everyone was out looking for her. "It was a just a small family disagreement," Margit said, swallowing hard. It would be so difficult to explain all of the details of Lilly's situation to this man. "You know how little children can be," she added, smiling sweetly.

The railway man scratched his head underneath his blue cap and frowned. "Well, I don't know," he said. "She doesn't look like she's too happy to see you. Are you sure she's family?"

Margit nodded firmly and stared hard at Lilly. "I'm sure. And our parents will be worried sick if I don't get her home."

Margit waited and held her breath. After a moment, the man shrugged his shoulders and dropped Lilly's hand. "All right," he said, "you take her. But, miss," he added, staring down at Lilly, "if I catch you here again, there's going to be trouble. Understand?"

"She understands," said Margit, grabbing Lilly by the hand before she had a chance to respond— or to run. "Thank you, sir."

Margit pulled Lilly from the lineup and moved across the hallway to an empty corner. Alice grabbed the suitcase and followed close behind. Lilly walked slowly and reluctantly, her eyes still lowered and her hand still clutching her photograph. Finally, away from the crowd of people, Margit turned to face Lilly.

"How could you run away without saying a word? You had us all so scared, Lilly," Margit began. "Mamma and Papa are sick with worry, and poor Jack thinks you'll never forgive him for what he did to your picture."

Lilly stared at the ground and said nothing.

"Please, Lilly," begged Margit. "You've got to say something."

Lilly lifted her head. Her eyes flashed with anger. "I miss my family," she whispered.

Margit nodded. "I know. I mean, I can't even begin to know how hard this is for you. I remember when I came here with Mamma, and we didn't know where Papa was, or if we would ever see him again. I didn't speak English, and I didn't have any friends. It took a long time to feel like I fit in, like I belonged here, or like anyone cared about me. But I had Mamma to help me, and I met Alice. Now I'm trying to help you, Lilly. We're all trying."

Did Lilly understand anything of what Margit was trying to say? The small girl stared down at her damaged picture.

"Jack's crazy about you," continued Margit.

"You know that, don't you? He would never do anything to hurt you."

Lilly looked up again, and this time tears were rolling slowly down her cheeks. The anger in her eyes had faded, replaced with sadness.

"I want to be your friend so badly," said Margit.

"We all do," added Alice, who stood close by.

"I know it's not the same as having your real family," said Margit, "but maybe you can start to think of us as your new family." She waited and watched Lilly.

Lilly reached over and pulled her suitcase from out of Alice's hand. Margit sighed, thinking that Lilly was going to walk away again. She had no words left to try and convince Lilly to stay. But instead of leaving, Lilly bent down and opened up her suitcase. She stared once more at the picture of her family, and slowly placed the photograph inside the small case. Then she closed the lid, locking the picture—and her past—inside. When she stood up and looked at Margit, her face was calm. She reached up and placed one hand in Margit's and the other in Alice's. Alice smiled and bent to pick up the suitcase once more.

"Let's go home," said Lilly.

Lilly reached over and pulled her suitcase from out of Alice's hand. Margit sighed, thinking that Lilly was going to walk away again.

Margit's parents were overjoyed to see Lilly enter their apartment, led by Margit. Mamma was the first to rush forward and gather Lilly in her arms.

"Oh, my poor sweet child," she murmured softly. "You have no idea how worried we were. We're so happy to have you back home with us." Mamma stroked Lilly's hair and kissed her gently on the forehead.

"You had us all so frightened," added Papa as he too came forward to hug Lilly. Lilly looked dwarfed in Papa's big embrace. In fact, she looked completely overwhelmed by the family's warmth and concern for her. She stood blinking her eyes and staring, first at Margit, then at Mamma and Papa, as if she were seeing them for the first time. It was as if she suddenly recognized that they truly cared for her, and she could begin to return their affection.

Jack was more hesitant. He crouched in a corner, his head buried deep in his arms. Margit had to coax and cajole him until he finally crept toward Lilly. Even then, he couldn't look up at her. He simply stood in front of Lilly, head bowed, looking quite miserable.

Lilly stared at Jack for the longest time. Finally, she reached out and took his chin in her hand, lifting it to meet her eyes. "Okay, Jack," Lilly said finally. "I'm not mad."

Jack could not believe what he was hearing. In fact, he stood for a minute longer, eyes opening wider and wider, until finally he hurled himself into Lilly's arms, nearly throwing her off balance. "Okay, Dibby!" Jack yelled. "Okay, okay!" Jack squeezed and squeezed and wouldn't let go. Mamma had to pry him off of her. Still, Jack remained at Lilly's side, reaching up to touch her arm every now and then, as if touching her confirmed that she had truly forgiven him.

Mamma and Papa asked few questions. They could see by the looks on Margit's and Lilly's faces that something had changed for the better. They would be able to get the details of Lilly's rescue later. But Papa knew that he had a few telephone calls to make.

"I need to call the police and tell them that you've found Lilly," said Papa. "And then I'd better call the lady from the Jewish Congress. I'll tell them that things seem to be better, yes?" he asked, looking in Lilly's direction.

Lilly nodded. "Yes," she said in a strong, clear voice.

"And I'm going to fix something to eat," added Mamma. "You must be starving, Lilly."

"I want to call Alice, too," said Margit, "just to let her know that everything is really okay."

When they had left Union Station, Alice had decided to return to her own home. "I think you and your family will have a lot to talk about," she had said. "You don't need me there."

Margit had nodded and swallowed hard. "Thank you," she whispered, hugging Alice, "for everything."

Alice smiled. "Will I see you tomorrow?"

"Of course," Margit replied. And she had meant it.

Papa was busy on the telephone, talking first with the police and then with Mrs. Wolfe from the Canadian Jewish Congress. Mamma headed for the kitchen to prepare what she called a "celebration feast." Jack was playing with Lilly, holding on to her and making her laugh. Margit took a small step back to watch her family. For the first time in weeks, she felt calm. It was as if a huge weight had been lifted from her shoulders. She knew that she still had Alice as her best friend. And she knew in her heart that things would work out between herself and Lilly. With these realizations, Margit felt at peace.

The doorbell rang, startling her. "I'll get it," she called as she ran for the door.

When Margit opened the door, Tom Simpson, the photographer from the *Toronto Telegram*, was standing there.

"Hello, young lady," Mr. Simpson said, tipping his hat and bowing slightly. "Mind if I come in? I'll just stay a minute, but I've got something for the young girl." He nodded toward Lilly, who had come to join Margit at the door.

Mr. Simpson entered the apartment and greeted Papa and Mamma, who emerged from the kitchen, her arms covered in flour. She wiped them quickly across her apron and shook hands with the reporter.

"I told you I'd be back," Mr. Simpson said. "I promised I'd bring you a copy of this." He reached into his pocket and pulled out a photograph. "It's for the young girl here."

Mr. Simpson handed the picture to Lilly as Margit's family crowded around. It was the picture that Mr. Simpson had taken in the apartment, a few days after Lilly's arrival. Mamma and Papa were posed at the back of the photo, with Lilly, Margit, and Jack in front. Lilly's hand rested lightly on Jack's shoulder. They looked like a typical loving family.

"Well, I guess I'll be going then," said Mr. Simpson awkwardly. The family was so mesmerized by the picture that no one said a word.

"Oh, pardon us all," said Mamma. "Please stay for tea."

Mr. Simpson shook his head. "No thanks, ma'am. I can see that you're all busy. I just wanted to bring the picture over for the girl."

Lilly looked up at Mr. Simpson and smiled, a warm, grateful smile. "Thank you," she said.

The reporter tipped his hat once more and turned to leave the apartment. When the door closed behind him, everyone turned to look at Lilly, waiting to see what she would do or say.

Lilly stared at the picture for another minute. Then she reached for her suitcase, opened it, and pulled out her family photograph, the one that Jack had drawn on, the one and only keepsake of her real family. She held the pictures side by side as Margit watched and held her breath. Then Lilly moved over to the couch and to the small table next to it. There she placed the two pictures beside one another. It was as if she now knew that there were two families that loved her: one that she would always hold in her memory, and one that was here for her now.

Jack ran to stand next to Lilly. "Okay, Dibby?" he asked, looking up at her.

Lilly smiled and nodded.

"We're here to stay, Lilly," said Margit, moving forward to place her arm around Lilly's shoulder. "Oh, and I promise I'll keep the crayons away from Jack!"

Author's Note

In this story, Lilly arrives in Toronto and immediately goes to live with Margit's family. In reality, the Jewish orphans who came to Toronto between 1947 and 1949 were initially housed at the Toronto Reception Centre, located in the former Jewish library at the corner of Harbord and Markham Streets. They stayed there for a period of observation before being allowed to go to live with families who were willing to house them. Not all of these children were placed with foster families. Many, especially the older ones, remained at the centre, where they were given room and board, went to school, and learned new skills and professions. Despite the fact that the war left these youngsters cautious and withdrawn, they were also resourceful and smart. The vast majority of Jewish orphans did well in Canada, and eventually grew to become fully contributing citizens with deep loyalty to this country.

ACKNOWLEDGEMENTS

IT HAS BEEN MY PLEASURE TO BREATHE LIFE INTO MARGIT AND TO DOCUMENT, THROUGH HER STORY, A VERY IMPORTANT TIME IN CANADIAN HISTORY. IT HAS BEEN AN HONOUR TO BE A PART OF THE OUR CANADIAN GIRL SERIES AND TO WORK WITH THE TALENTED AND DEDICATED STAFF AT PENGUIN GROUP (CANADA).

THANKS TO BARBARA BERSON FOR HER COMMITMENT, SUPPORT, AND FRIENDSHIP. THANKS AS WELL TO SANDRA TOOZE AND STEPHANIE FYSH FOR THEIR CREATIVE AND EDITORIAL INPUT. JANET WILSON CREATED A VISUAL IMAGE OF MARGIT THAT I LOVE. THANKS FOR THE ARTISTRY. A SPECIAL THANK-YOU AS WELL TO DOROTA GLOWACKA FOR HELPING WITH THE POLISH TRANSLATIONS.

MY LOVE AND GRATITUDE TO MY FRIENDS AND FAMILY, ESPECIALLY MY HUSBAND, IAN EPSTEIN, AND MY CHILDREN, GABI AND JAKE.

Dear Reader,

This has been the fourth and final book about Margit. We hope you've enjoyed meeting and getting to know her as much as we have enjoyed bringing her—and her wonderful story—to you.

Although Margit's tale is told, there are still eleven more terrific girls to read about, whose exciting adventures take place in Canada's past—girls just like you. So do keep on reading!

And please—don't forget to keep in touch! We love receiving your incredible letters telling us about your favourite stories and which girls you like best. And thank you for telling us about the stories you would like to read! There are so many remarkable stories in Canadian history. It seems that wherever we live, great stories live too, in our towns and cities, on our rivers and mountains. We hope that Our Canadian Girl captures the richness of that past.

Sincerely,
Barbara Berson
Editor

Canada's

1608
Samuel de Champlain establishes the first fortified trading post at Quebec.

1759
The British defeat the French in the Battle of the Plains of Abraham.

1812
The United States declares war against Canada.

1845
The expedition of Sir John Franklin to the Arctic ends when the ship is frozen in the pack ice; the fate of its crew remains a mystery.

1869
Louis Riel leads his Metis followers in the Red River Rebellion.

1871
British Columbia joins Canada.

1755
The British expel the entire French population of Acadia (today's Maritime provinces), sending them into exile.

1776
The 13 Colonies revolt against Britain, and the Loyalists flee to Canada.

1762
Elizabeth

1837
Calling for responsible government, the Patriotes, following Louis-Joseph Papineau, rebel in Lower Canada; William Lyon Mackenzie leads the uprising in Upper Canada.

1867
New Brunswick, Nova Scotia, and the United Province of Canada come together in Confederation to form the Dominion of Canada.

1870
Manitoba joins Canada. The Northwest Territories become an official territory of Canada.

1862
Lisa

Timeline

1885
At Craigellachie, British Columbia, the last spike is driven to complete the building of the Canadian Pacific Railway.

1898
The Yukon Territory becomes an official territory of Canada.

1914
Britain declares war on Germany, and Canada, because of its ties to Britain, is at war too.

1918
As a result of the Wartime Elections Act, the women of Canada are given the right to vote in federal elections.

1945
World War II ends conclusively with the dropping of atomic bombs on Hiroshima and Nagasaki.

1873
Prince Edward Island joins Canada.

1896
Gold is discovered on Bonanza Creek, a tributary of the Klondike River.

1905
Alberta and Saskatchewan join Canada.

1917
In the Halifax harbour, two ships collide, causing an explosion that leaves more than 1,600 dead and 9,000 injured.

1939
Canada declares war on Germany seven days after war is declared by Britain and France.

1949
Newfoundland, under the leadership of Joey Smallwood, joins Canada.

1897
Emily

1947
Margit